P9-CDP-051

J FIC Van

Van Lente, F.
The creeping doom.

PRICE: $25.63 (3559/by   )

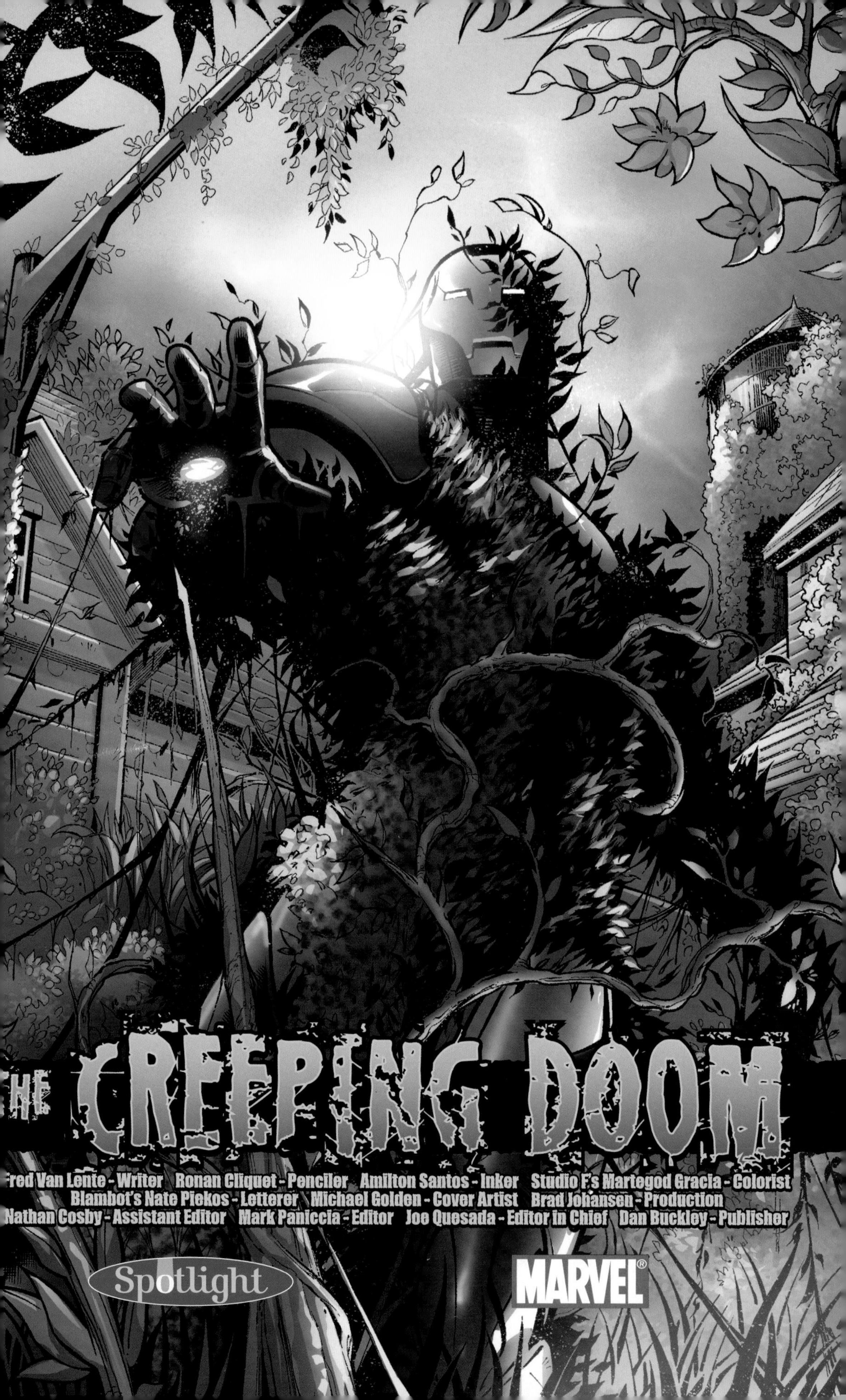
HE CREEPING DOOM
red Van Lente - Writer Ronan Cliquet - Penciler Amilton Santos - Inker Studio F's Martegod Gracia - Colorist
Blambot's Nate Piekos - Letterer Michael Golden - Cover Artist Brad Johansen - Production
Nathan Cosby - Assistant Editor Mark Paniccia - Editor Joe Quesada - Editor in Chief Dan Buckley - Publisher
Spotlight
MARVEL®

VISIT US AT
www.abdopublishing.com

Reinforced library bound edition published in 2009 by Spotlight, a division of the ABDO Publishing Group, 8000 West 78th Street, Edina, Minnesota 55439. Spotlight produces high-quality reinforced library bound editions for schools and libraries. Published by agreement with Marvel Characters, Inc.

MARVEL, and all related character names and the distinctive likenesses thereof are trademarks of Marvel Characters, Inc., and is/are used with permission. Copyright © 2008 Marvel Characters, Inc. All rights reserved. www.marvel.com

MARVEL, Iron Man: TM & © 2008 Marvel Characters, Inc. All rights reserved. www.marvel.com. This book is produced under license from Marvel Characters, Inc.

Library of Congress Cataloging-in-Publication Data

Van Lente, Fred.
  The creeping doom / Fred Van Lente, writer ; Ronan Cliquet, penciler ; Amilton Santos, inker ; Martegod Gracia, colorist ; Nate Piekos, letterer. -- Reinforced library bound ed.
     p. cm. -- (Iron Man)
  "Marvel."
  ISBN 978-1-59961-551-6
  1. Graphic novels. [1. Graphic novels.] I. Cliquet, Ronan, ill. II. Title.
  PZ7.7.V26Cre 2008
  [E]--dc22
                                    2008000106

All Spotlight books have reinforced library bindings and
are manufactured in the United States of America.

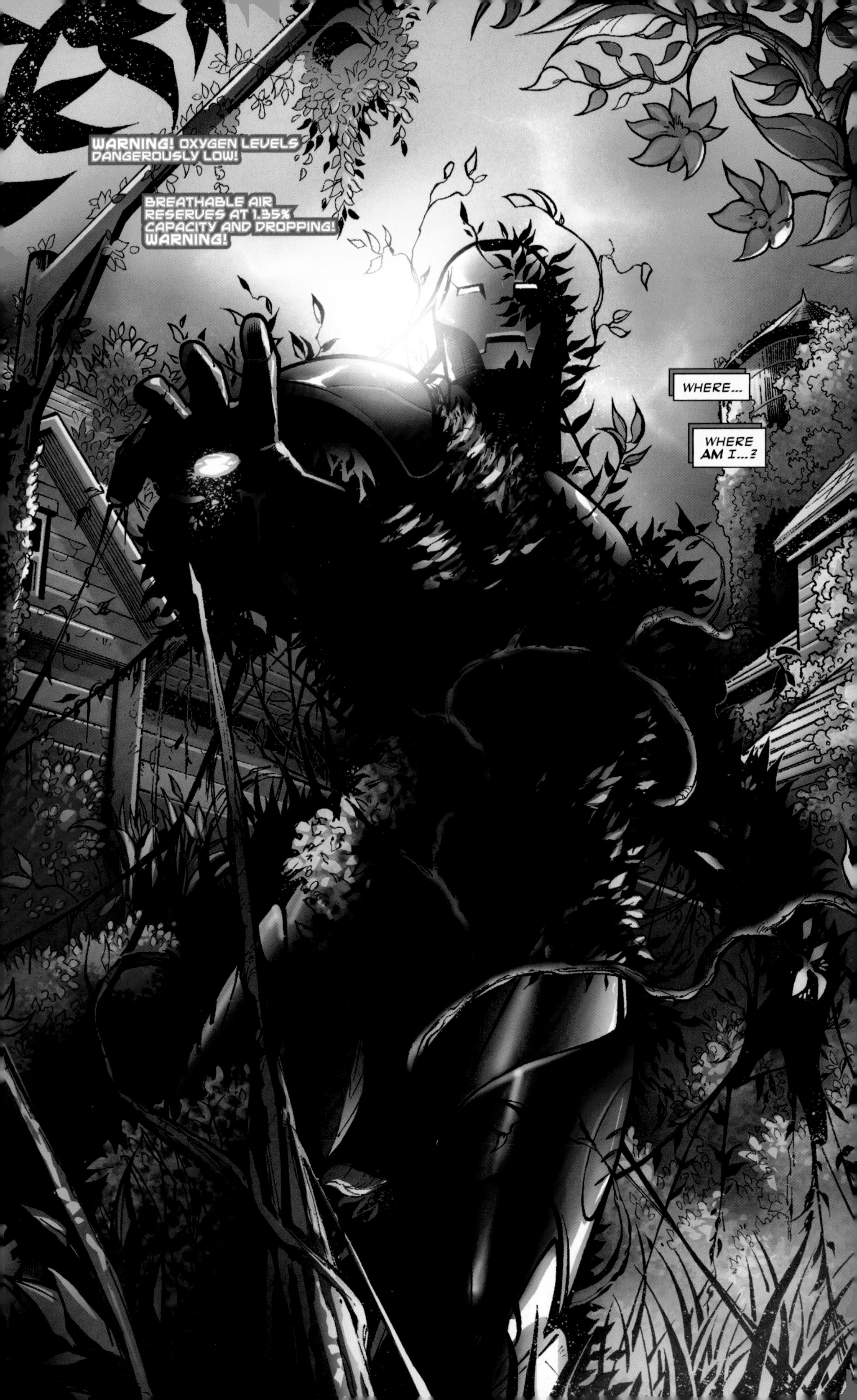
WARNING! OXYGEN LEVELS DANGEROUSLY LOW!
BREATHABLE AIR RESERVES AT 1.35% CAPACITY AND DROPPING! WARNING!
WHERE...
WHERE AM I...?

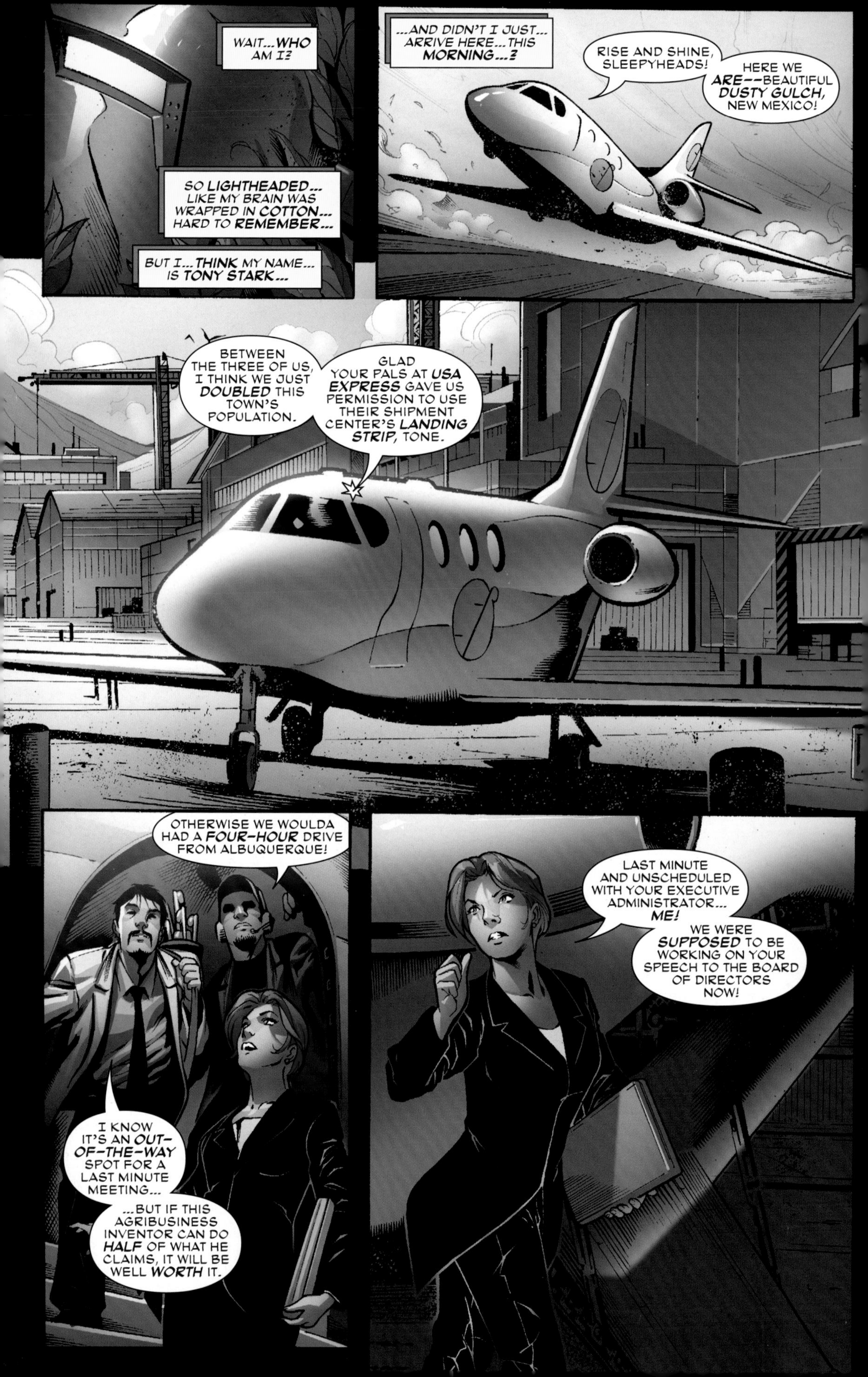
WAIT...WHO AM I?
SO LIGHTHEADED... LIKE MY BRAIN WAS WRAPPED IN COTTON... HARD TO REMEMBER...
BUT I...THINK MY NAME... IS TONY STARK...
...AND DIDN'T I JUST... ARRIVE HERE... THIS MORNING...?
RISE AND SHINE, SLEEPYHEADS!
HERE WE ARE--BEAUTIFUL DUSTY GULCH, NEW MEXICO!
BETWEEN THE THREE OF US, I THINK WE JUST DOUBLED THIS TOWN'S POPULATION.
GLAD YOUR PALS AT USA EXPRESS GAVE US PERMISSION TO USE THEIR SHIPMENT CENTER'S LANDING STRIP, TONE.
OTHERWISE WE WOULDA HAD A FOUR-HOUR DRIVE FROM ALBUQUERQUE!
I KNOW IT'S AN OUT-OF-THE-WAY SPOT FOR A LAST MINUTE MEETING...
...BUT IF THIS AGRIBUSINESS INVENTOR CAN DO HALF OF WHAT HE CLAIMS, IT WILL BE WELL WORTH IT.
LAST MINUTE AND UNSCHEDULED WITH YOUR EXECUTIVE ADMINISTRATOR... ME!
WE WERE SUPPOSED TO BE WORKING ON YOUR SPEECH TO THE BOARD OF DIRECTORS NOW!

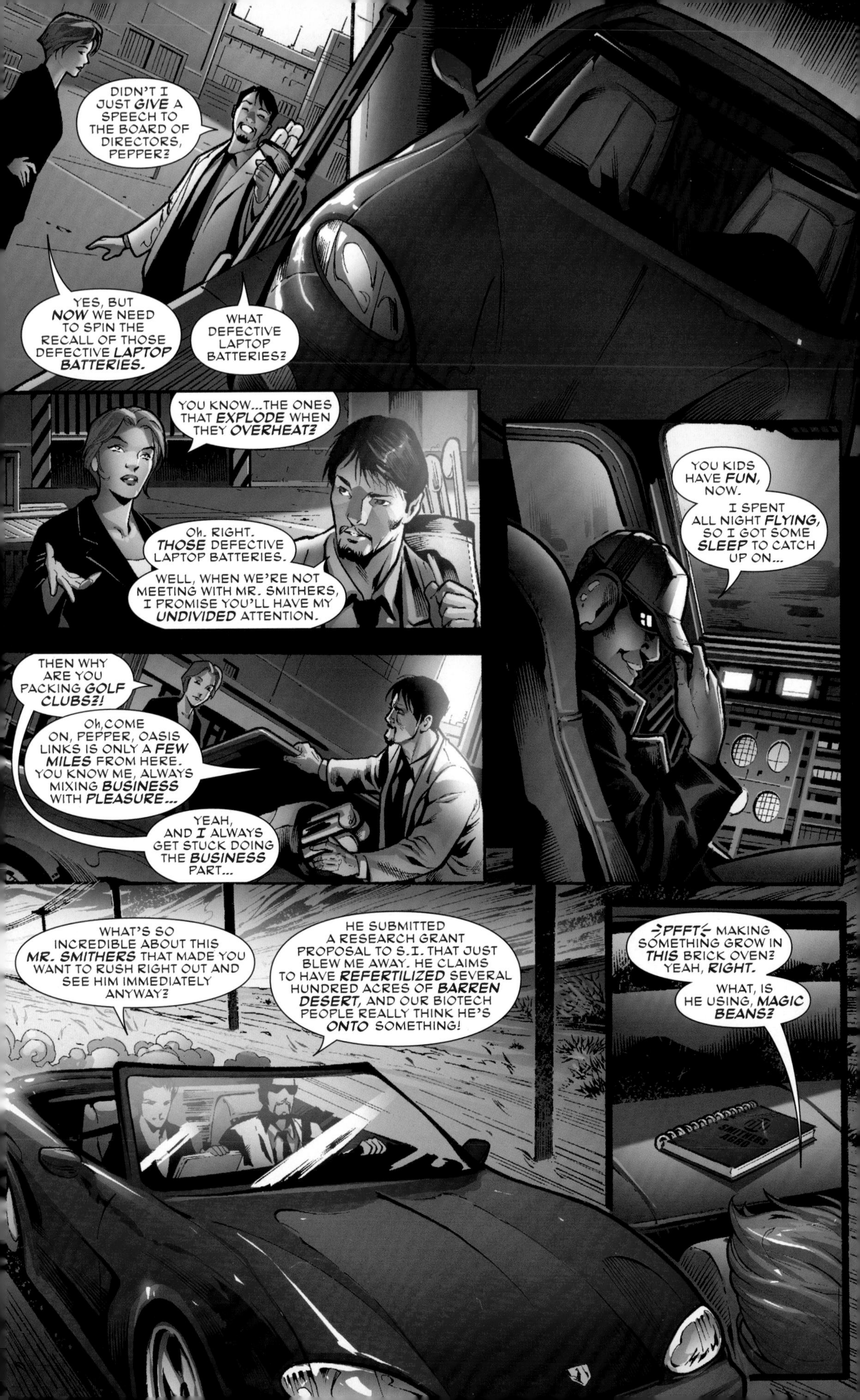
DIDN'T I JUST GIVE A SPEECH TO THE BOARD OF DIRECTORS, PEPPER?
YES, BUT NOW WE NEED TO SPIN THE RECALL OF THOSE DEFECTIVE LAPTOP BATTERIES.
WHAT DEFECTIVE LAPTOP BATTERIES?
YOU KNOW...THE ONES THAT EXPLODE WHEN THEY OVERHEAT?
Oh. RIGHT. THOSE DEFECTIVE LAPTOP BATTERIES.
WELL, WHEN WE'RE NOT MEETING WITH MR. SMITHERS, I PROMISE YOU'LL HAVE MY UNDIVIDED ATTENTION.
YOU KIDS HAVE FUN, NOW.
I SPENT ALL NIGHT FLYING, SO I GOT SOME SLEEP TO CATCH UP ON...
THEN WHY ARE YOU PACKING GOLF CLUBS?!
Oh, COME ON, PEPPER, OASIS LINKS IS ONLY A FEW MILES FROM HERE. YOU KNOW ME, ALWAYS MIXING BUSINESS WITH PLEASURE...
YEAH, AND I ALWAYS GET STUCK DOING THE BUSINESS PART...
WHAT'S SO INCREDIBLE ABOUT THIS MR. SMITHERS THAT MADE YOU WANT TO RUSH RIGHT OUT AND SEE HIM IMMEDIATELY ANYWAY?
HE SUBMITTED A RESEARCH GRANT PROPOSAL TO S.I. THAT JUST BLEW ME AWAY. HE CLAIMS TO HAVE REFERTILIZED SEVERAL HUNDRED ACRES OF BARREN DESERT, AND OUR BIOTECH PEOPLE REALLY THINK HE'S ONTO SOMETHING!
PFFT MAKING SOMETHING GROW IN THIS BRICK OVEN? YEAH, RIGHT.
WHAT, IS HE USING, MAGIC BEANS?
SMITHERS AGRO

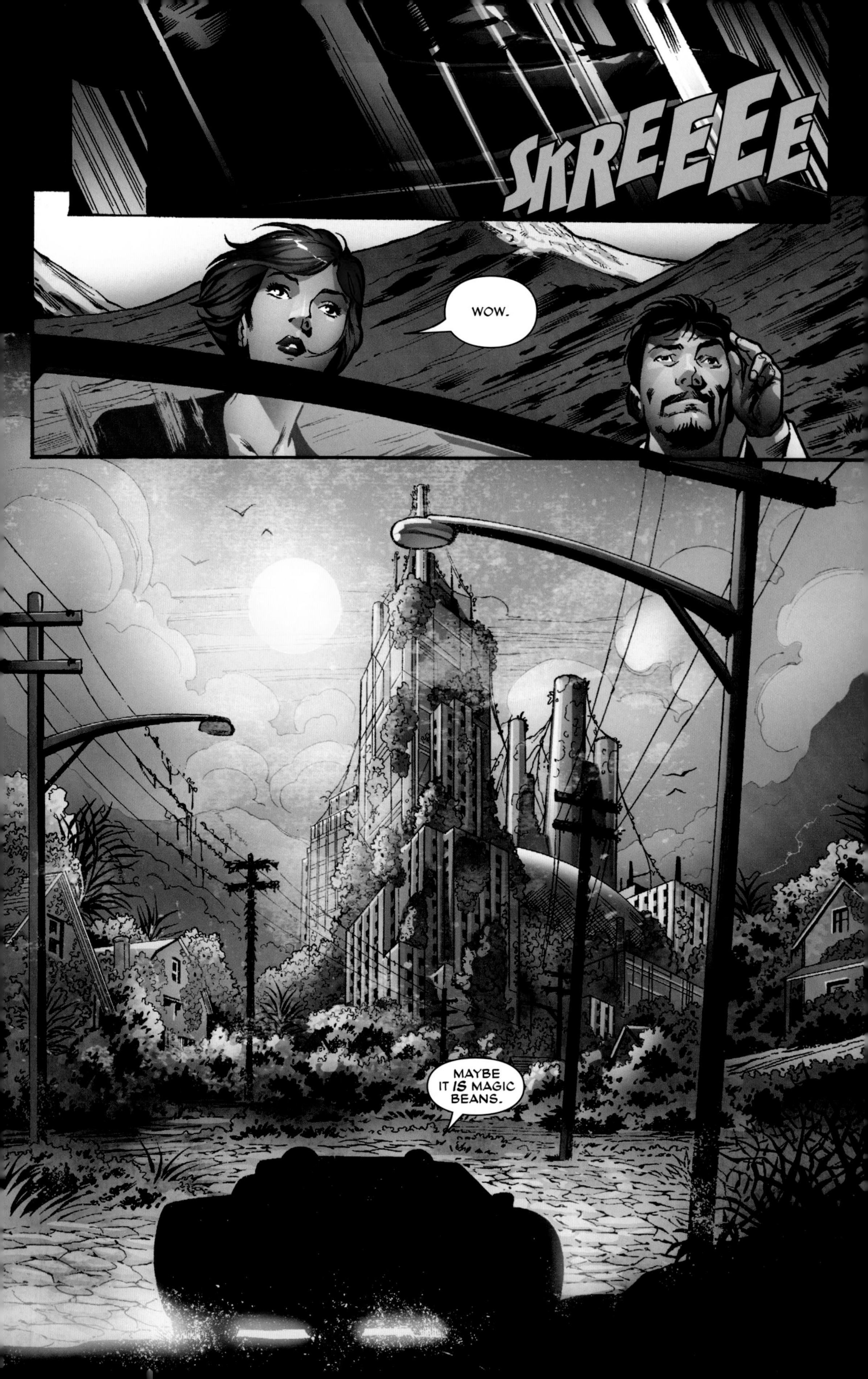
SKREEEE
WOW.
MAYBE IT IS MAGIC BEANS.

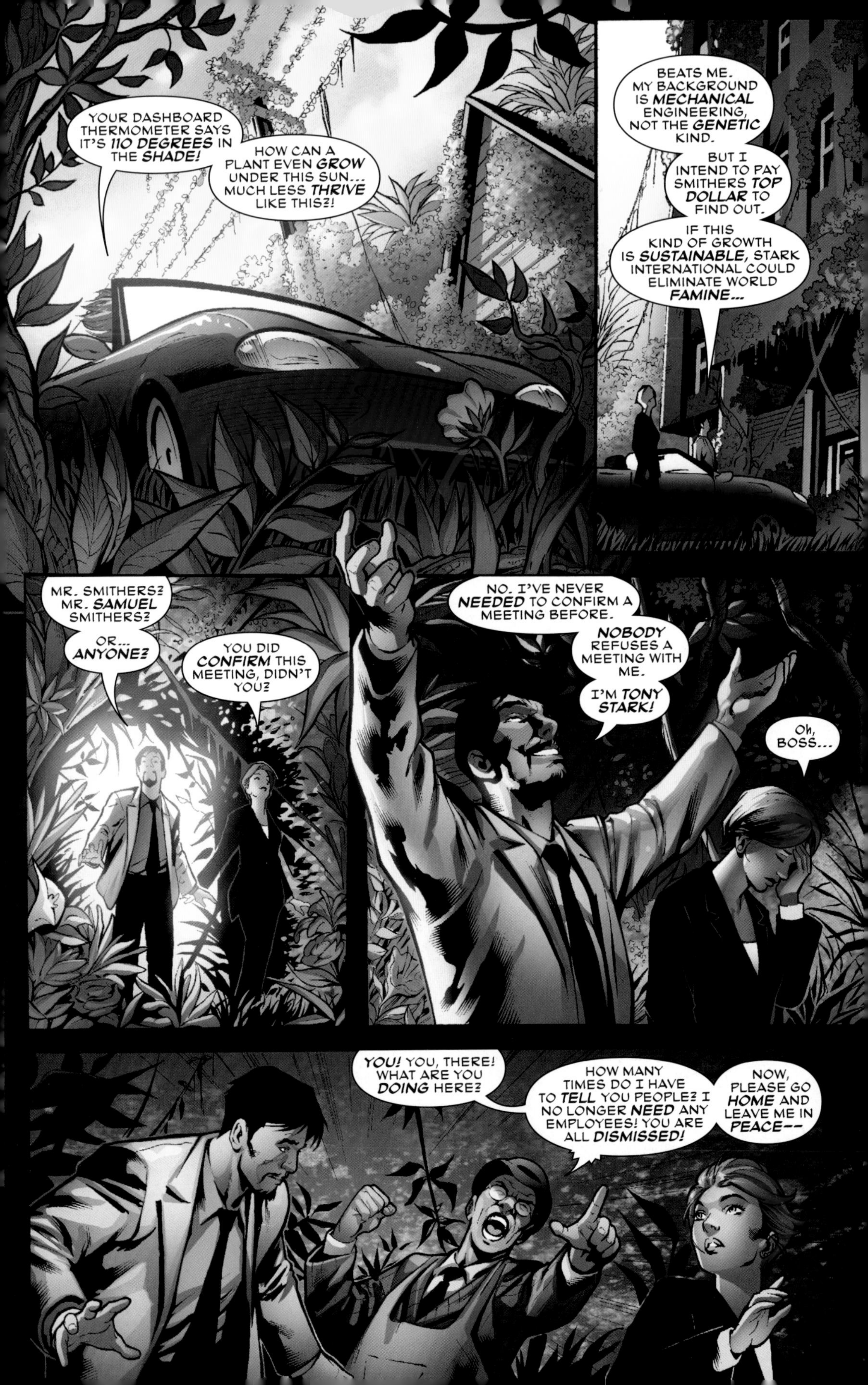
YOUR DASHBOARD THERMOMETER SAYS IT'S 110 DEGREES IN THE SHADE!
HOW CAN A PLANT EVEN GROW UNDER THIS SUN... MUCH LESS THRIVE LIKE THIS?!
BEATS ME. MY BACKGROUND IS MECHANICAL ENGINEERING, NOT THE GENETIC KIND.
BUT I INTEND TO PAY SMITHERS TOP DOLLAR TO FIND OUT.
IF THIS KIND OF GROWTH IS SUSTAINABLE, STARK INTERNATIONAL COULD ELIMINATE WORLD FAMINE...
MR. SMITHERS? MR. SAMUEL SMITHERS?
OR... ANYONE?
YOU DID CONFIRM THIS MEETING, DIDN'T YOU?
NO. I'VE NEVER NEEDED TO CONFIRM A MEETING BEFORE.
NOBODY REFUSES A MEETING WITH ME.
I'M TONY STARK!
Oh, BOSS...
YOU! YOU, THERE! WHAT ARE YOU DOING HERE?
HOW MANY TIMES DO I HAVE TO TELL YOU PEOPLE? I NO LONGER NEED ANY EMPLOYEES! YOU ARE ALL DISMISSED!
NOW, PLEASE GO HOME AND LEAVE ME IN PEACE--

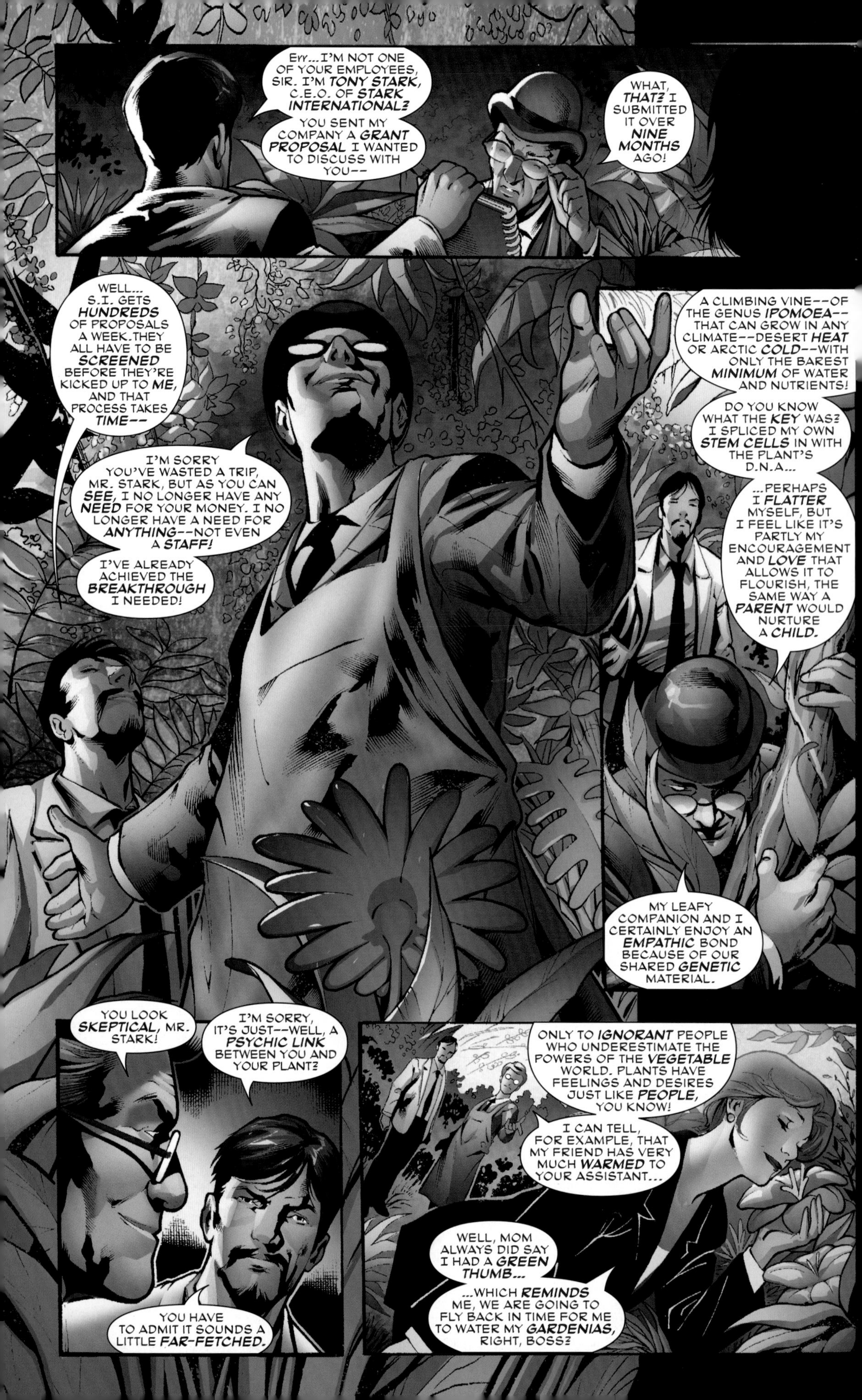

ERR... I'M NOT ONE OF YOUR EMPLOYEES, SIR. I'M TONY STARK, C.E.O. OF STARK INTERNATIONAL?
YOU SENT MY COMPANY A GRANT PROPOSAL I WANTED TO DISCUSS WITH YOU--
WHAT, THAT? I SUBMITTED IT OVER NINE MONTHS AGO!
WELL... S.I. GETS HUNDREDS OF PROPOSALS A WEEK. THEY ALL HAVE TO BE SCREENED BEFORE THEY'RE KICKED UP TO ME, AND THAT PROCESS TAKES TIME--
I'M SORRY YOU'VE WASTED A TRIP, MR. STARK, BUT AS YOU CAN SEE, I NO LONGER HAVE ANY NEED FOR YOUR MONEY. I NO LONGER HAVE A NEED FOR ANYTHING--NOT EVEN A STAFF!
I'VE ALREADY ACHIEVED THE BREAKTHROUGH I NEEDED!
A CLIMBING VINE--OF THE GENUS IPOMOEA--THAT CAN GROW IN ANY CLIMATE--DESERT HEAT OR ARCTIC COLD--WITH ONLY THE BAREST MINIMUM OF WATER AND NUTRIENTS!
DO YOU KNOW WHAT THE KEY WAS? I SPLICED MY OWN STEM CELLS IN WITH THE PLANT'S D.N.A...
...PERHAPS I FLATTER MYSELF, BUT I FEEL LIKE IT'S PARTLY MY ENCOURAGEMENT AND LOVE THAT ALLOWS IT TO FLOURISH, THE SAME WAY A PARENT WOULD NURTURE A CHILD.
MY LEAFY COMPANION AND I CERTAINLY ENJOY AN EMPATHIC BOND BECAUSE OF OUR SHARED GENETIC MATERIAL.
YOU LOOK SKEPTICAL, MR. STARK!
I'M SORRY, IT'S JUST--WELL, A PSYCHIC LINK BETWEEN YOU AND YOUR PLANT?
YOU HAVE TO ADMIT IT SOUNDS A LITTLE FAR-FETCHED.
ONLY TO IGNORANT PEOPLE WHO UNDERESTIMATE THE POWERS OF THE VEGETABLE WORLD. PLANTS HAVE FEELINGS AND DESIRES JUST LIKE PEOPLE, YOU KNOW!
I CAN TELL, FOR EXAMPLE, THAT MY FRIEND HAS VERY MUCH WARMED TO YOUR ASSISTANT...
WELL, MOM ALWAYS DID SAY I HAD A GREEN THUMB...
...WHICH REMINDS ME, WE ARE GOING TO FLY BACK IN TIME FOR ME TO WATER MY GARDENIAS, RIGHT, BOSS?

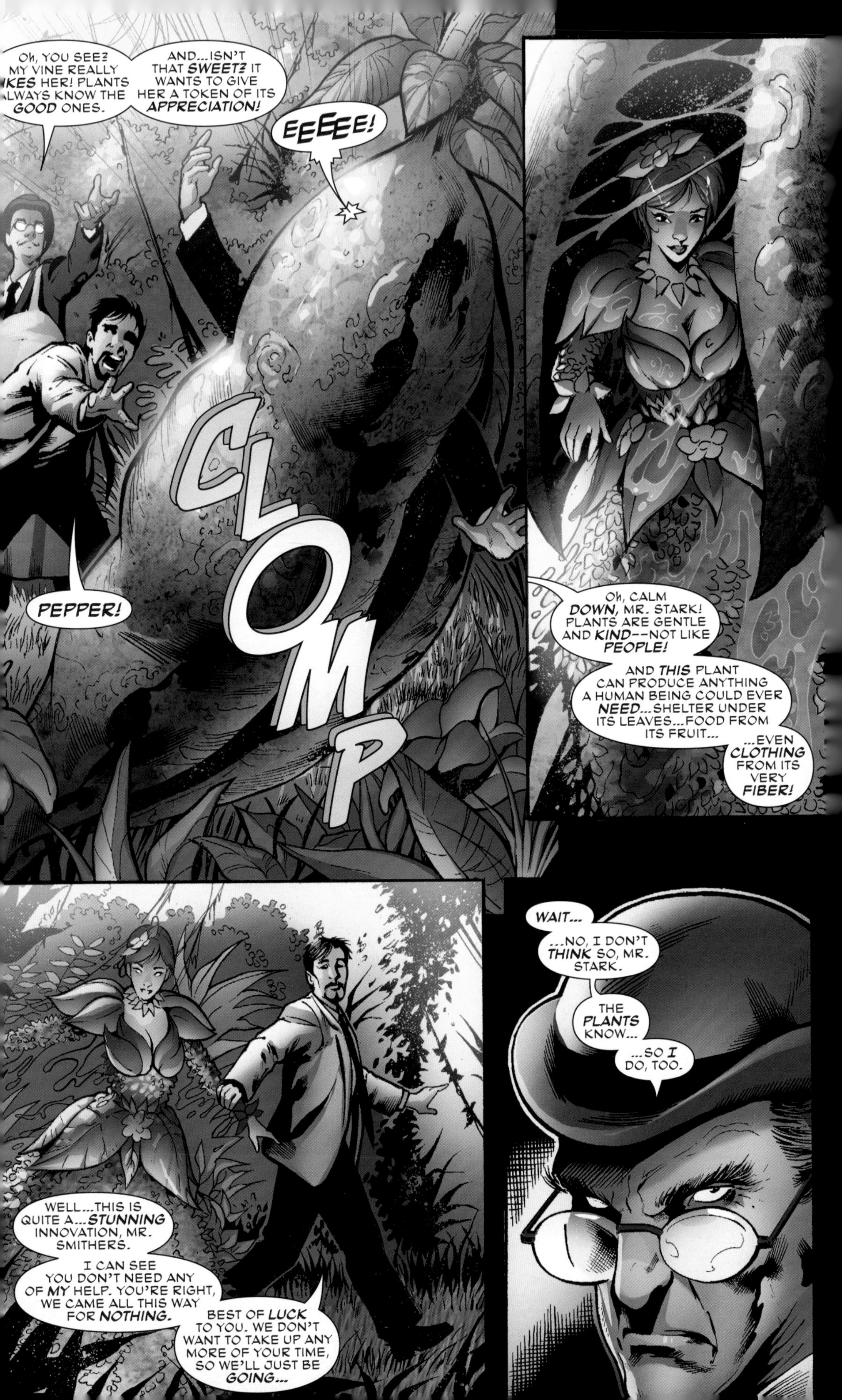

OH, YOU SEE? MY VINE REALLY LIKES HER! PLANTS ALWAYS KNOW THE GOOD ONES.
AND...ISN'T THAT SWEET? IT WANTS TO GIVE HER A TOKEN OF ITS APPRECIATION!
EEEEE!
CLOMP
PEPPER!
OH, CALM DOWN, MR. STARK! PLANTS ARE GENTLE AND KIND--NOT LIKE PEOPLE!
AND THIS PLANT CAN PRODUCE ANYTHING A HUMAN BEING COULD EVER NEED...SHELTER UNDER ITS LEAVES...FOOD FROM ITS FRUIT...
...EVEN CLOTHING FROM ITS VERY FIBER!
WELL...THIS IS QUITE A...STUNNING INNOVATION, MR. SMITHERS.
I CAN SEE YOU DON'T NEED ANY OF MY HELP. YOU'RE RIGHT, WE CAME ALL THIS WAY FOR NOTHING.
BEST OF LUCK TO YOU. WE DON'T WANT TO TAKE UP ANY MORE OF YOUR TIME, SO WE'LL JUST BE GOING...
WAIT...
...NO, I DON'T THINK SO, MR. STARK.
THE PLANTS KNOW...
...SO I DO, TOO.

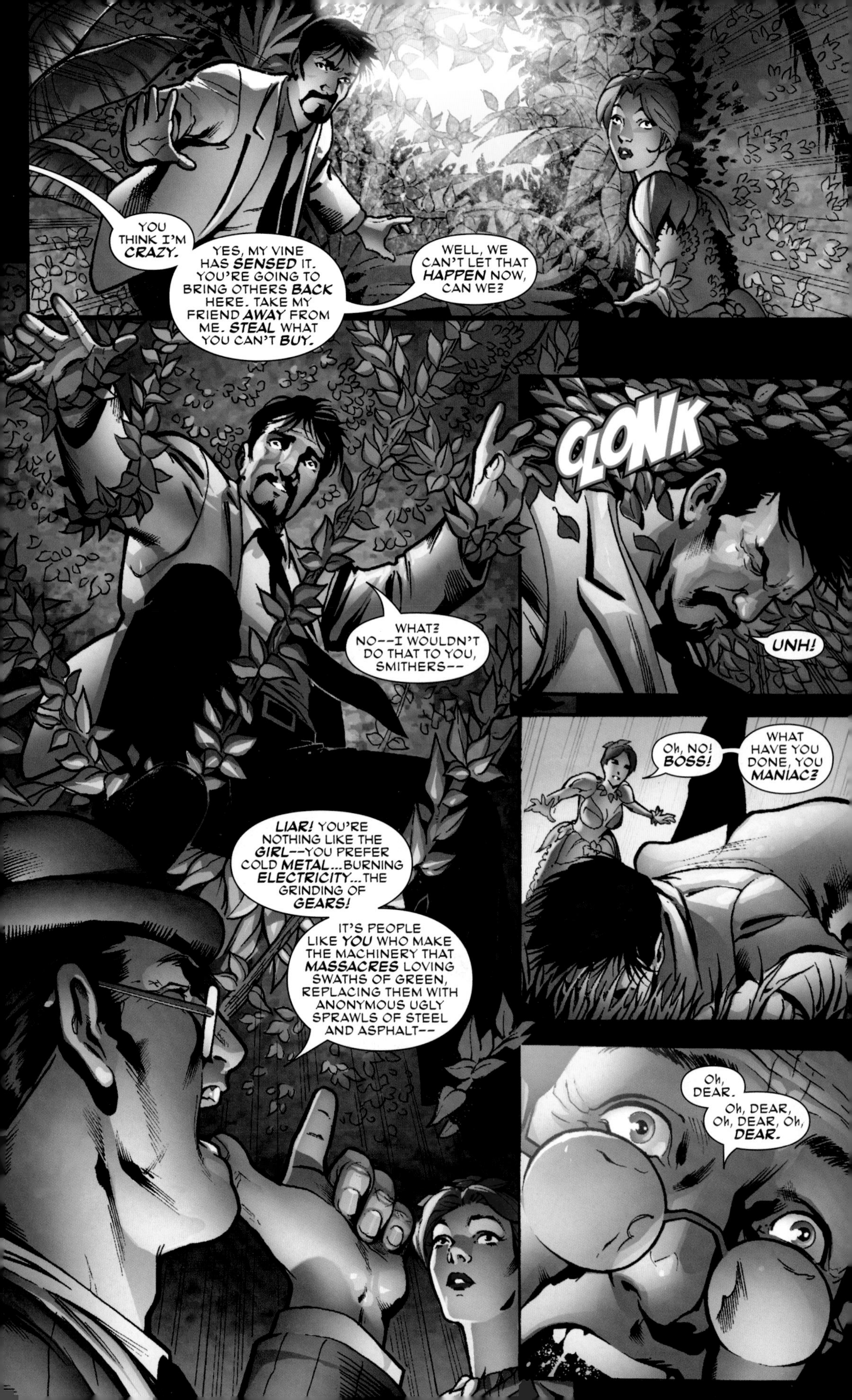
YOU THINK I'M CRAZY.
YES, MY VINE HAS SENSED IT. YOU'RE GOING TO BRING OTHERS BACK HERE. TAKE MY FRIEND AWAY FROM ME. STEAL WHAT YOU CAN'T BUY.
WELL, WE CAN'T LET THAT HAPPEN NOW, CAN WE?
WHAT? NO--I WOULDN'T DO THAT TO YOU, SMITHERS--
LIAR! YOU'RE NOTHING LIKE THE GIRL--YOU PREFER COLD METAL...BURNING ELECTRICITY...THE GRINDING OF GEARS!
IT'S PEOPLE LIKE YOU WHO MAKE THE MACHINERY THAT MASSACRES LOVING SWATHS OF GREEN, REPLACING THEM WITH ANONYMOUS UGLY SPRAWLS OF STEEL AND ASPHALT--
CLONK
UNH!
Oh, NO! BOSS!
WHAT HAVE YOU DONE, YOU MANIAC?
Oh, DEAR.
Oh, DEAR, Oh, DEAR, Oh, DEAR.

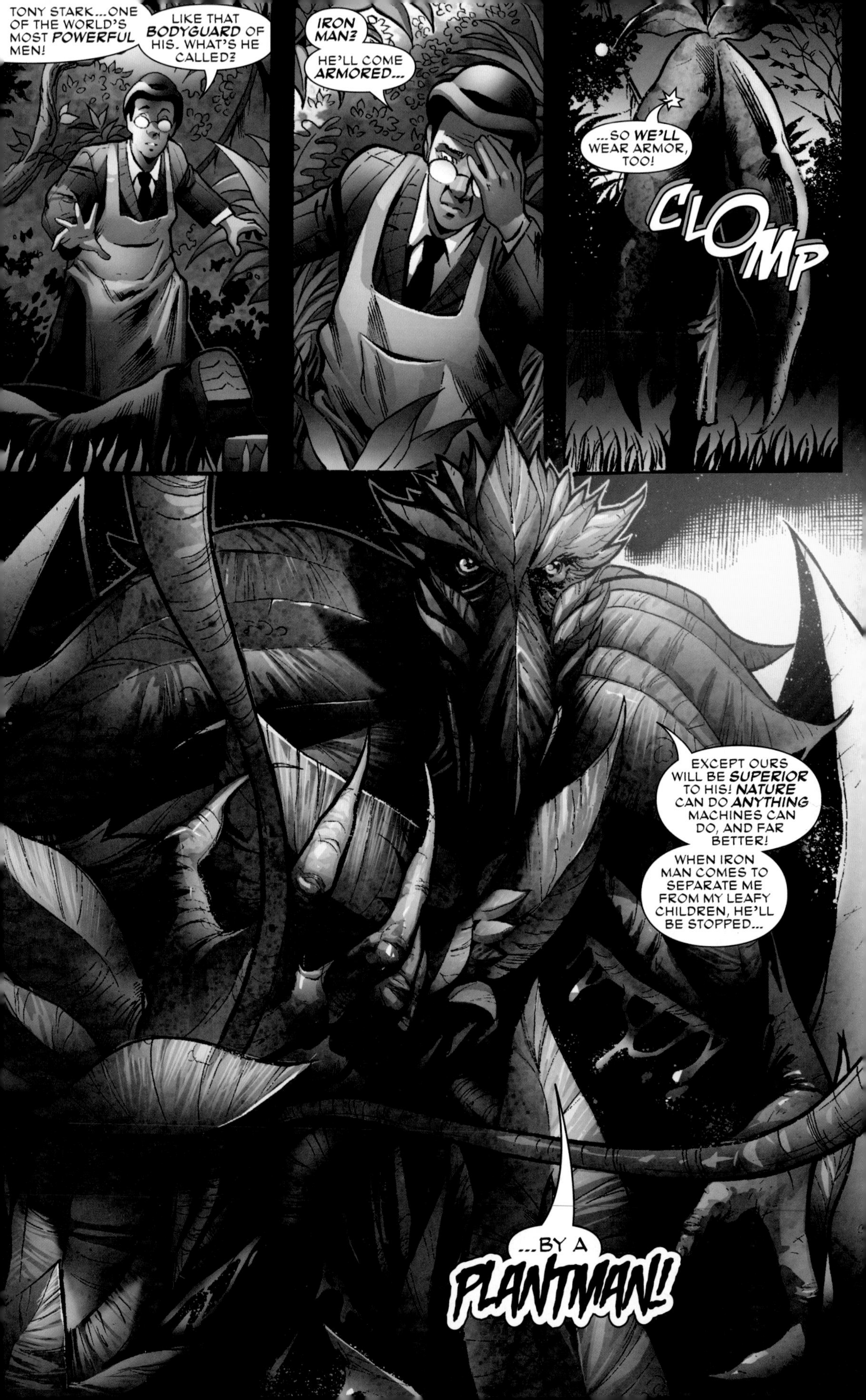

TONY STARK...ONE OF THE WORLD'S MOST POWERFUL MEN!
LIKE THAT BODYGUARD OF HIS. WHAT'S HE CALLED?
IRON MAN?
HE'LL COME ARMORED...
...SO WE'LL WEAR ARMOR, TOO!
CLOMP
EXCEPT OURS WILL BE SUPERIOR TO HIS! NATURE CAN DO ANYTHING MACHINES CAN DO, AND FAR BETTER!
WHEN IRON MAN COMES TO SEPARATE ME FROM MY LEAFY CHILDREN, HE'LL BE STOPPED...
...BY A PLANTMAN!

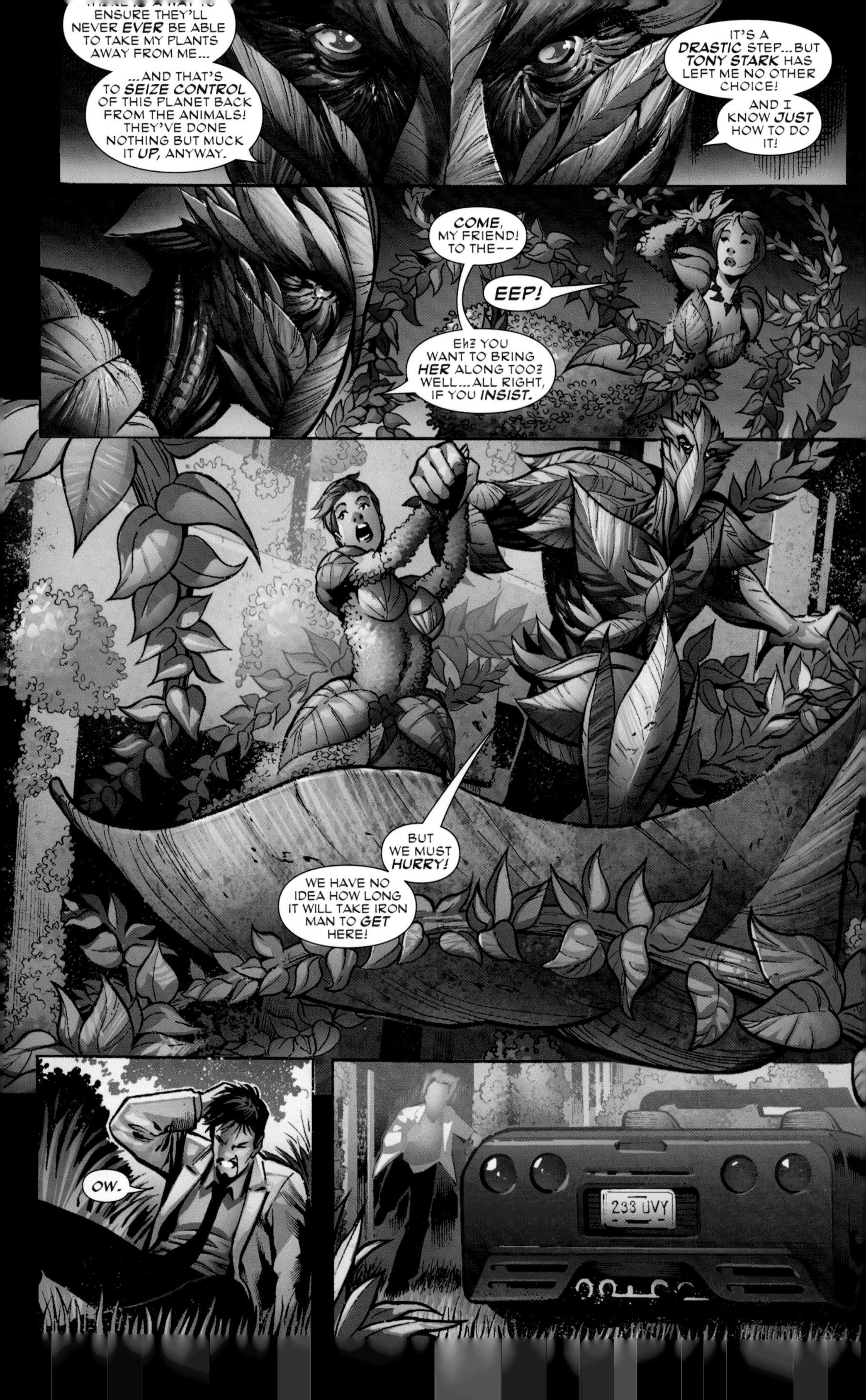
ENSURE THEY'LL NEVER EVER BE ABLE TO TAKE MY PLANTS AWAY FROM ME...
...AND THAT'S TO SEIZE CONTROL OF THIS PLANET BACK FROM THE ANIMALS! THEY'VE DONE NOTHING BUT MUCK IT UP, ANYWAY.
IT'S A DRASTIC STEP...BUT TONY STARK HAS LEFT ME NO OTHER CHOICE!
AND I KNOW JUST HOW TO DO IT!
COME, MY FRIEND! TO THE--
EEP!
EH? YOU WANT TO BRING HER ALONG TOO? WELL...ALL RIGHT, IF YOU INSIST.
BUT WE MUST HURRY!
WE HAVE NO IDEA HOW LONG IT WILL TAKE IRON MAN TO GET HERE!
OW.
233 UVY

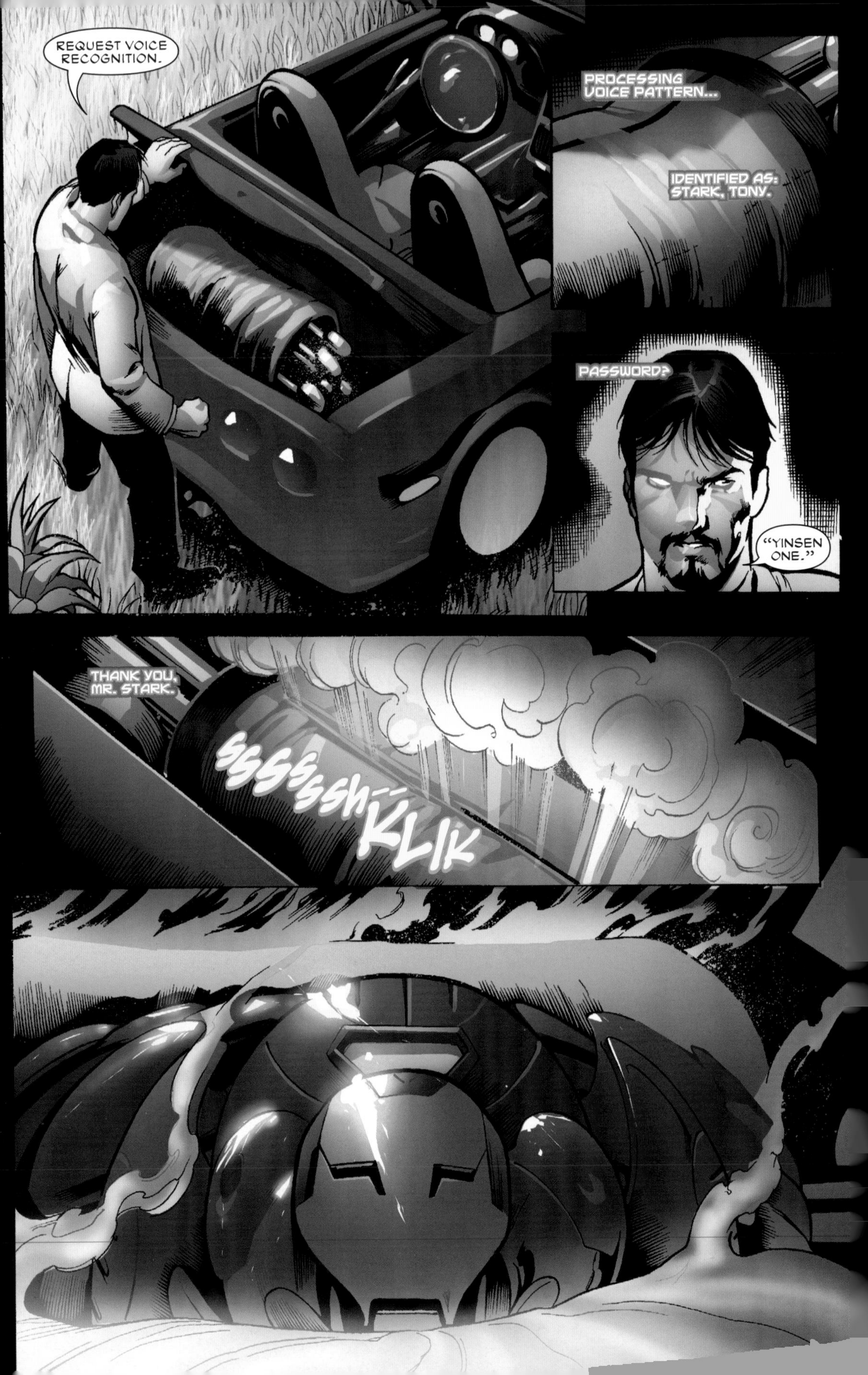

REQUEST VOICE RECOGNITION.
PROCESSING VOICE PATTERN...
IDENTIFIED AS: STARK, TONY.
PASSWORD?
"YINSEN ONE."
THANK YOU, MR. STARK.
SSSSSSH--KLIK

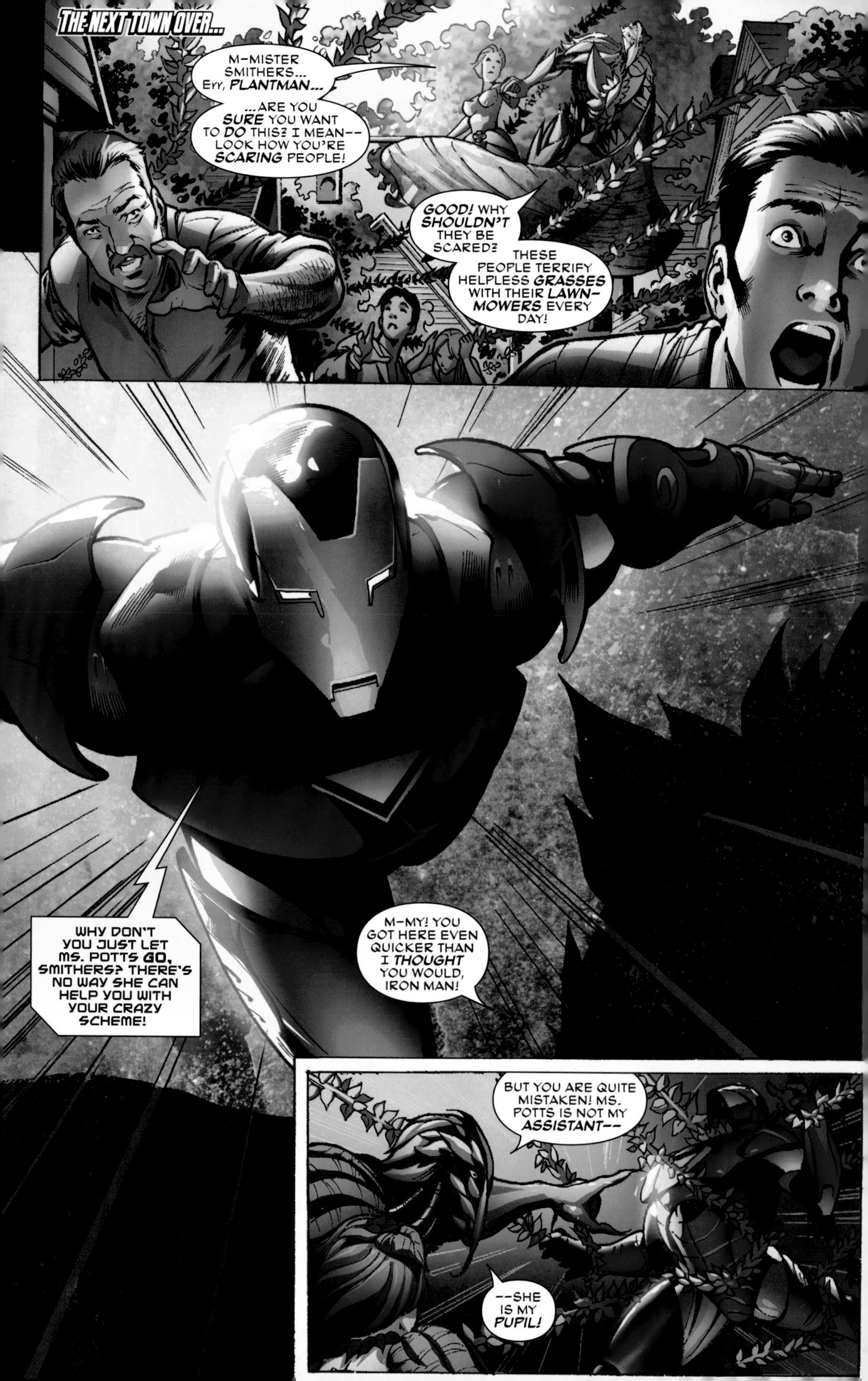
THE NEXT TOWN OVER...
M-MISTER SMITHERS... ERR, PLANTMAN...
...ARE YOU SURE YOU WANT TO DO THIS? I MEAN-- LOOK HOW YOU'RE SCARING PEOPLE!
GOOD! WHY SHOULDN'T THEY BE SCARED?
THESE PEOPLE TERRIFY HELPLESS GRASSES WITH THEIR LAWN-MOWERS EVERY DAY!
WHY DON'T YOU JUST LET MS. POTTS GO, SMITHERS? THERE'S NO WAY SHE CAN HELP YOU WITH YOUR CRAZY SCHEME!
M-MY! YOU GOT HERE EVEN QUICKER THAN I THOUGHT YOU WOULD, IRON MAN!
BUT YOU ARE QUITE MISTAKEN! MS. POTTS IS NOT MY ASSISTANT--
--SHE IS MY PUPIL!

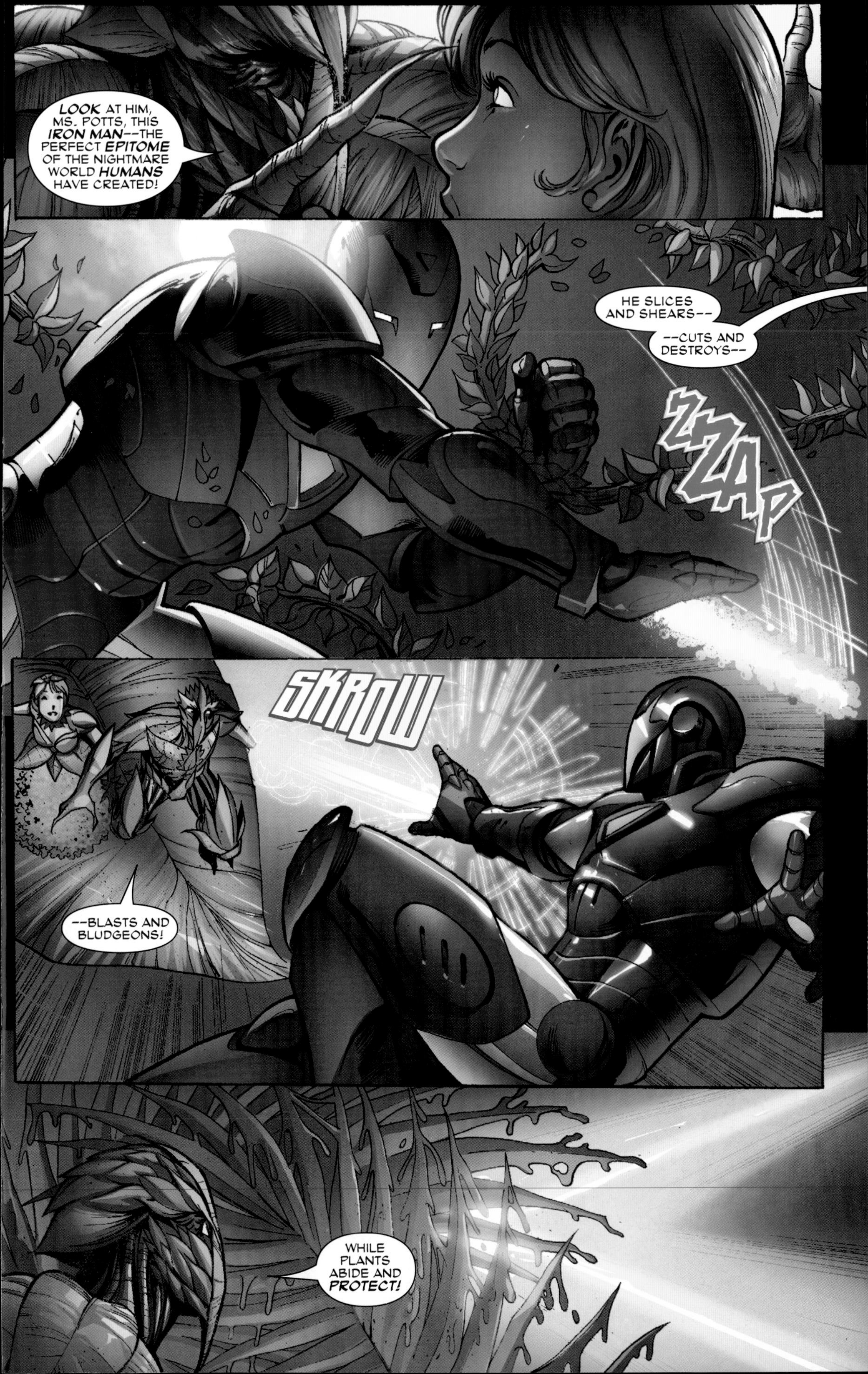
LOOK AT HIM, MS. POTTS, THIS IRON MAN--THE PERFECT EPITOME OF THE NIGHTMARE WORLD HUMANS HAVE CREATED!
HE SLICES AND SHEARS--
--CUTS AND DESTROYS--
ZZZAP
SKROW
--BLASTS AND BLUDGEONS!
WHILE PLANTS ABIDE AND PROTECT!

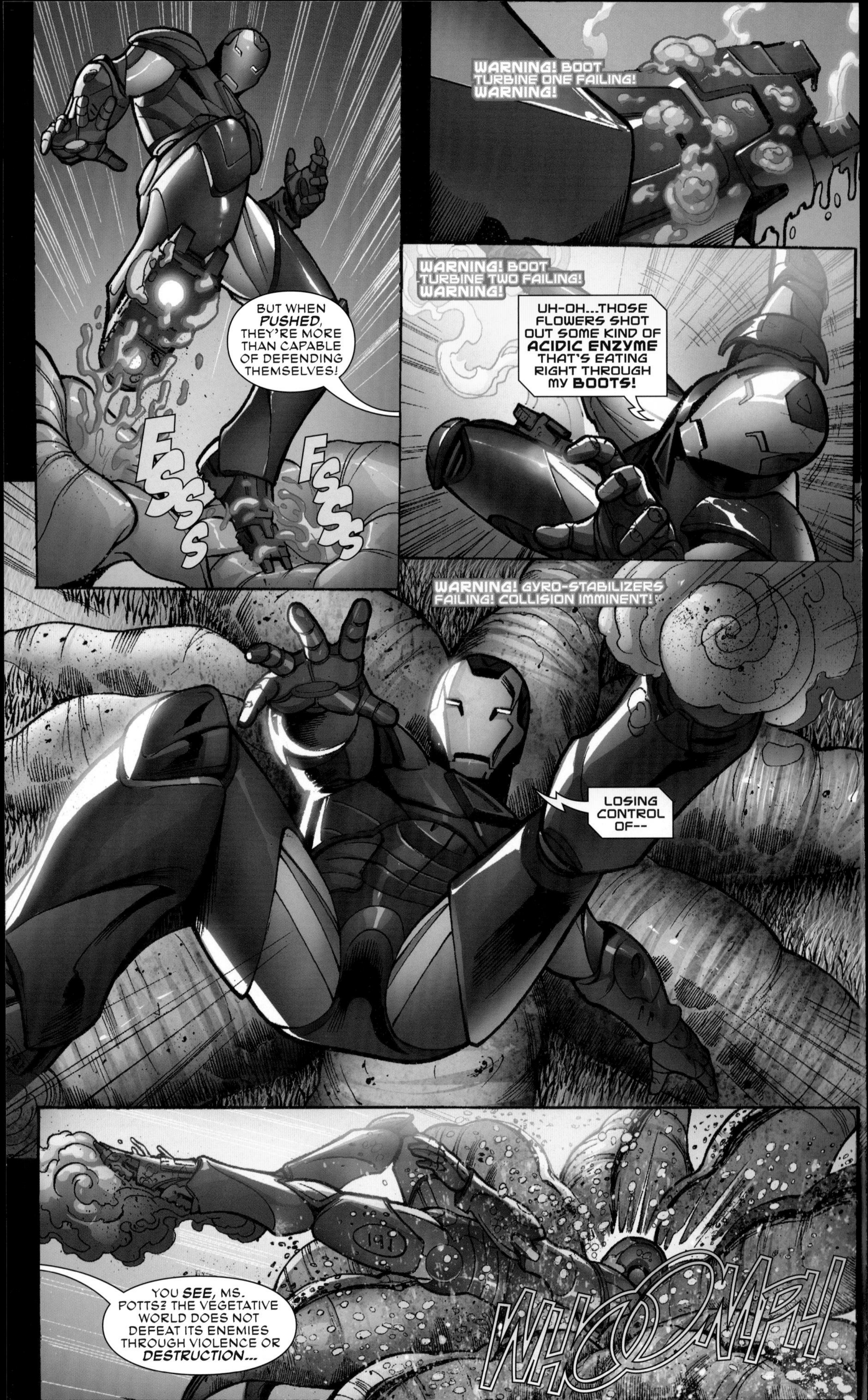
BUT WHEN PUSHED, THEY'RE MORE THAN CAPABLE OF DEFENDING THEMSELVES!
FSSSS
FSSSS
WARNING! BOOT TURBINE ONE FAILING! WARNING!
WARNING! BOOT TURBINE TWO FAILING! WARNING!
UH-OH...THOSE FLOWERS SHOT OUT SOME KIND OF ACIDIC ENZYME THAT'S EATING RIGHT THROUGH MY BOOTS!
WARNING! GYRO-STABILIZERS FAILING! COLLISION IMMINENT!
LOSING CONTROL OF--
YOU SEE, MS. POTTS? THE VEGETATIVE WORLD DOES NOT DEFEAT ITS ENEMIES THROUGH VIOLENCE OR DESTRUCTION...
WHOOMPH

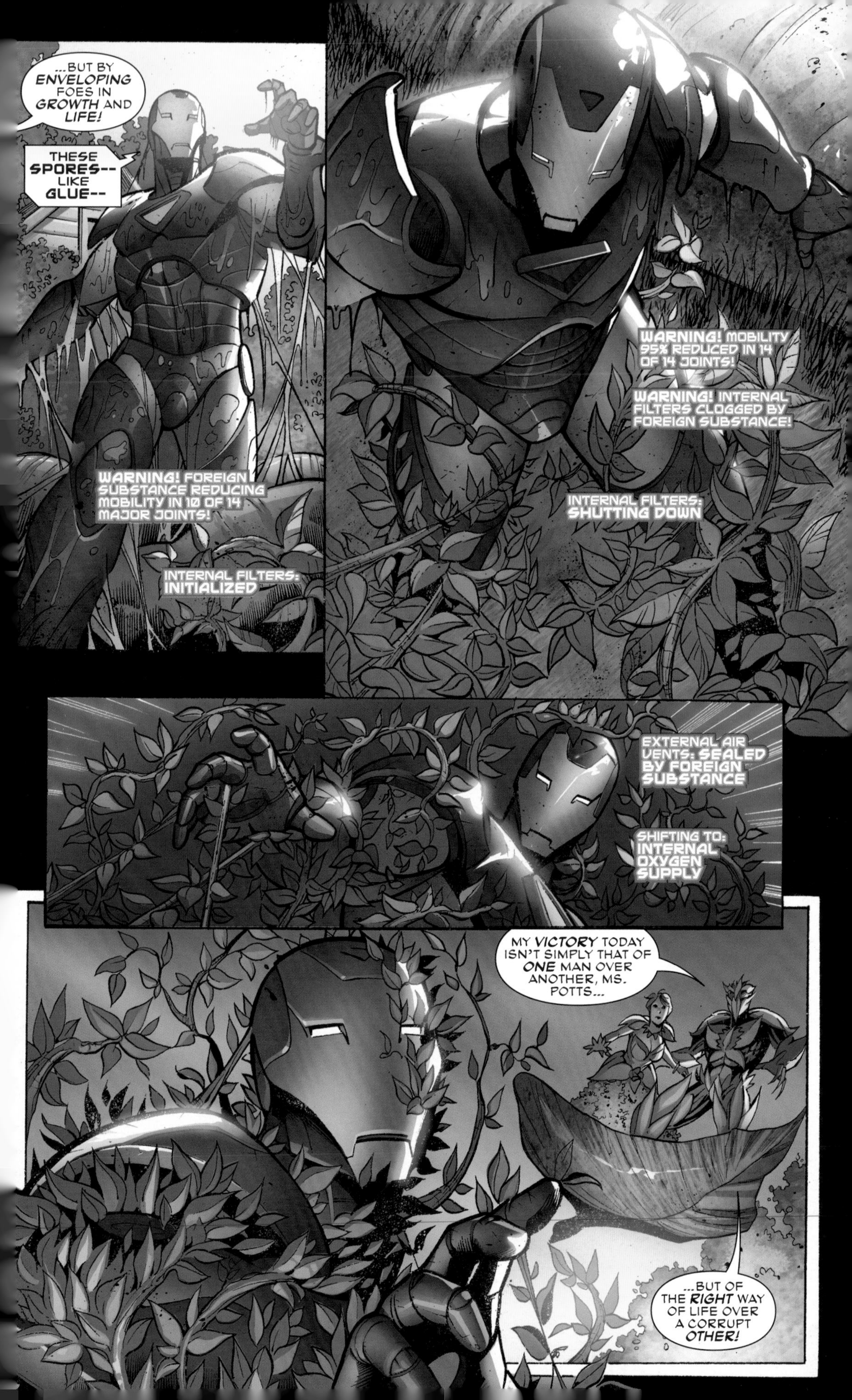
...BUT BY ENVELOPING FOES IN GROWTH AND LIFE!
THESE SPORES-- LIKE GLUE--
WARNING! FOREIGN SUBSTANCE REDUCING MOBILITY IN 10 OF 14 MAJOR JOINTS!
INTERNAL FILTERS: INITIALIZED
WARNING! MOBILITY 95% REDUCED IN 14 OF 14 JOINTS!
WARNING! INTERNAL FILTERS CLOGGED BY FOREIGN SUBSTANCE!
INTERNAL FILTERS: SHUTTING DOWN
EXTERNAL AIR VENTS: SEALED BY FOREIGN SUBSTANCE
SHIFTING TO: INTERNAL OXYGEN SUPPLY
MY VICTORY TODAY ISN'T SIMPLY THAT OF ONE MAN OVER ANOTHER, MS. POTTS...
...BUT OF THE RIGHT WAY OF LIFE OVER A CORRUPT OTHER!

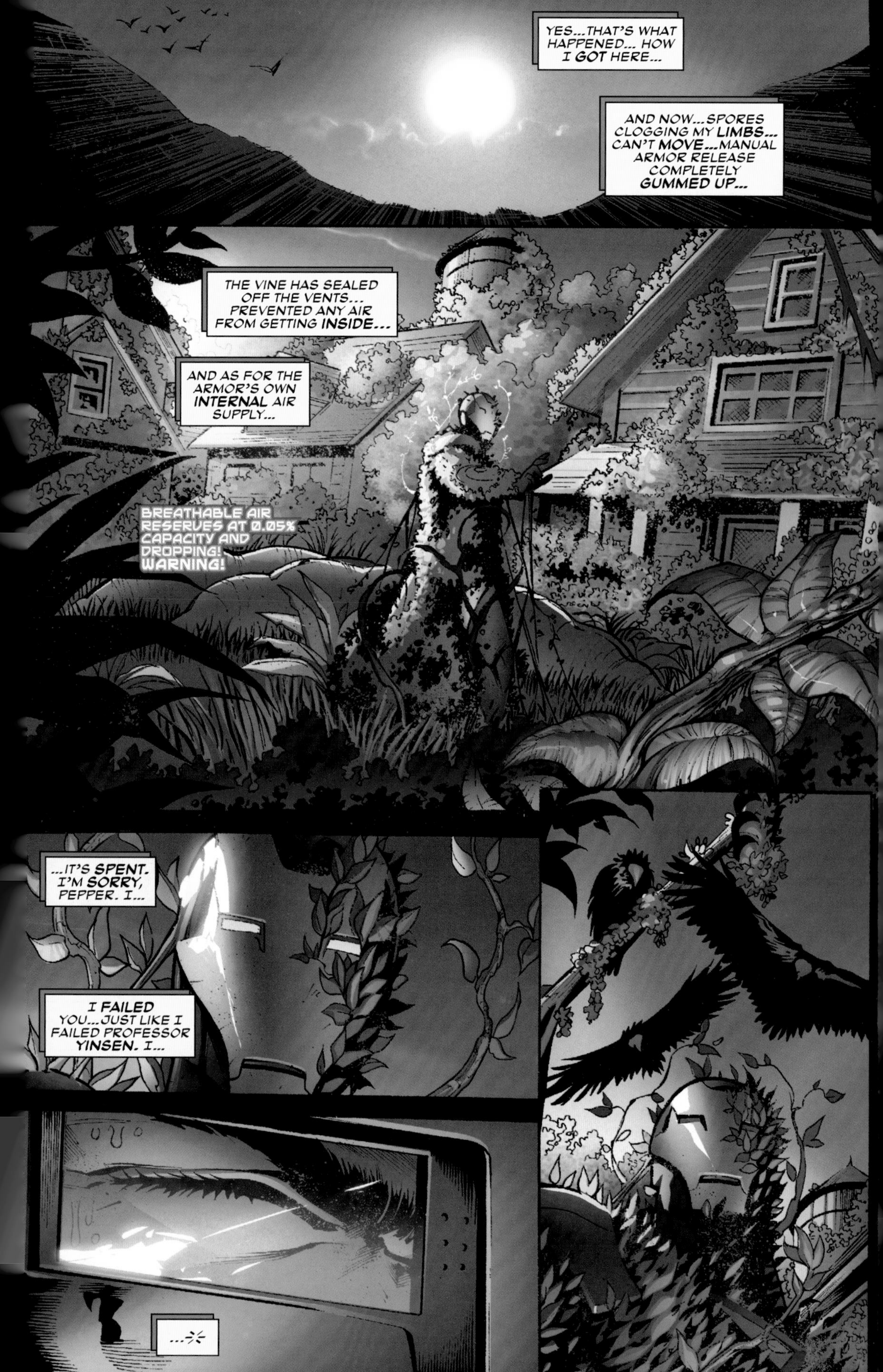
YES...THAT'S WHAT HAPPENED... HOW I GOT HERE...
AND NOW...SPORES CLOGGING MY LIMBS... CAN'T MOVE...MANUAL ARMOR RELEASE COMPLETELY GUMMED UP...
THE VINE HAS SEALED OFF THE VENTS... PREVENTED ANY AIR FROM GETTING INSIDE...
AND AS FOR THE ARMOR'S OWN INTERNAL AIR SUPPLY...
BREATHABLE AIR RESERVES AT 0.05% CAPACITY AND DROPPING! WARNING!
...IT'S SPENT. I'M SORRY, PEPPER. I...
I FAILED YOU...JUST LIKE I FAILED PROFESSOR YINSEN. I...
...

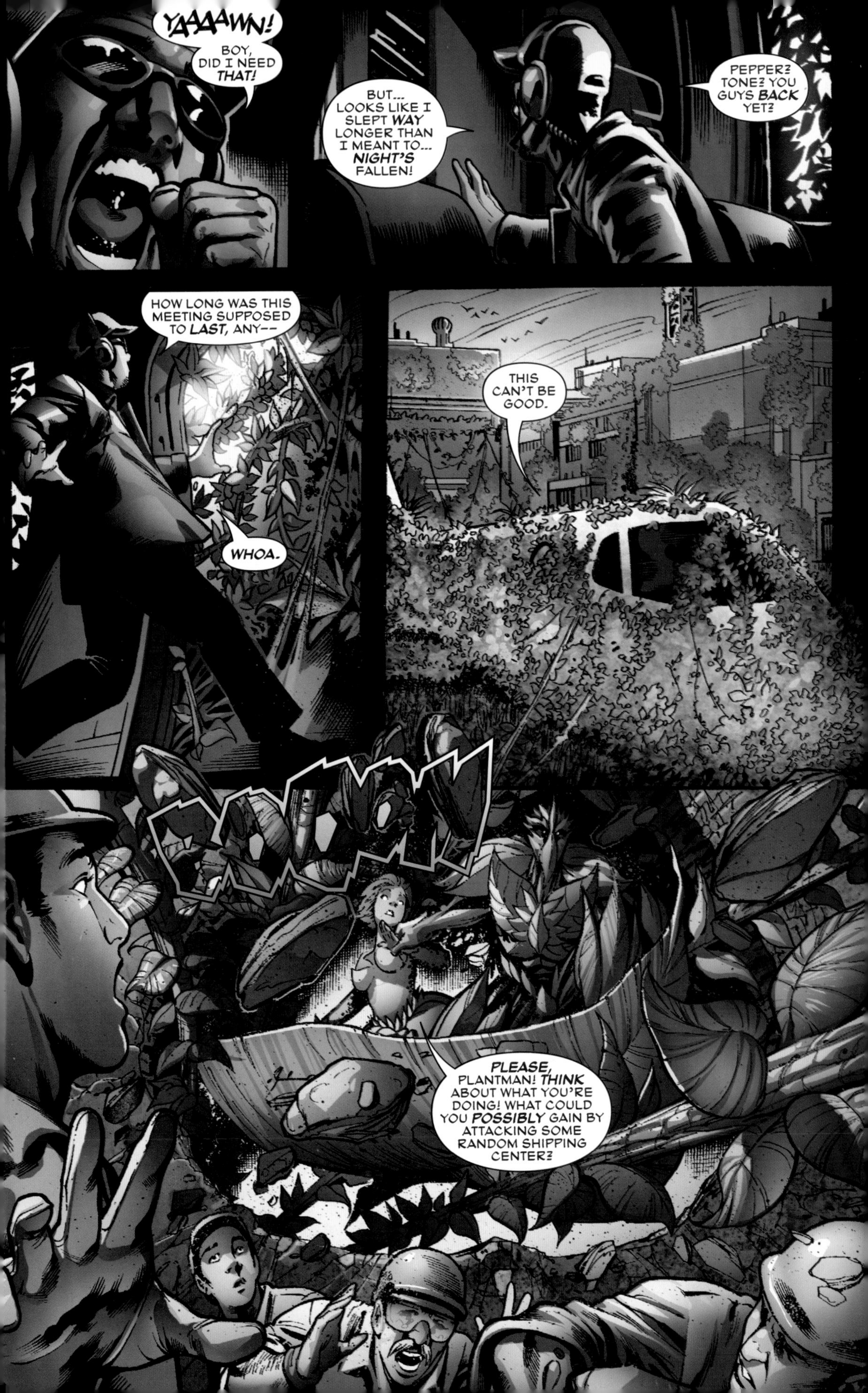
YAAAAWN!
BOY, DID I NEED THAT!
BUT... LOOKS LIKE I SLEPT WAY LONGER THAN I MEANT TO... NIGHT'S FALLEN!
PEPPER? TONE? YOU GUYS BACK YET?
HOW LONG WAS THIS MEETING SUPPOSED TO LAST, ANY--
WHOA.
THIS CAN'T BE GOOD.
PLEASE, PLANTMAN! THINK ABOUT WHAT YOU'RE DOING! WHAT COULD YOU POSSIBLY GAIN BY ATTACKING SOME RANDOM SHIPPING CENTER?

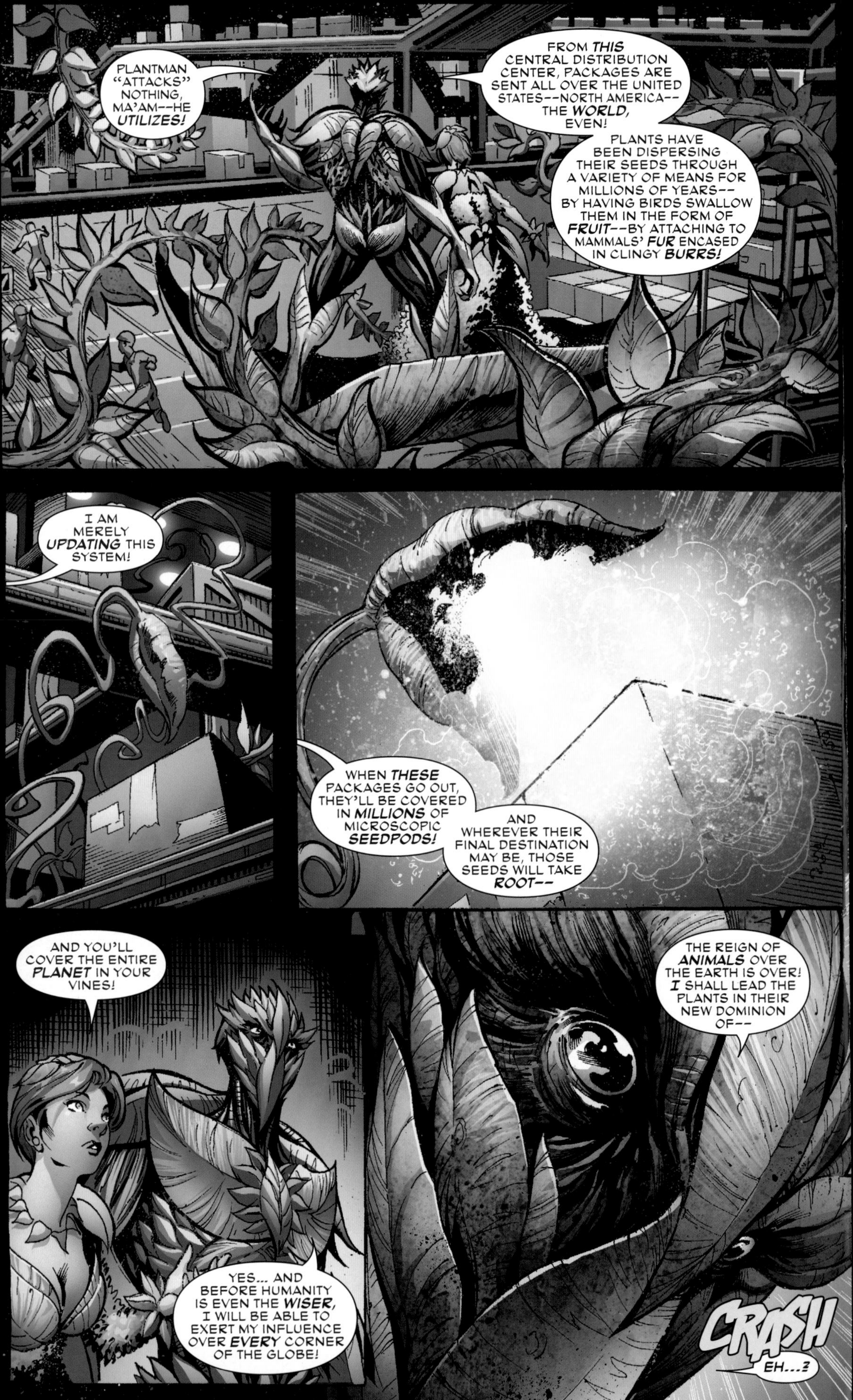
PLANTMAN "ATTACKS" NOTHING, MA'AM--HE UTILIZES!
FROM THIS CENTRAL DISTRIBUTION CENTER, PACKAGES ARE SENT ALL OVER THE UNITED STATES--NORTH AMERICA--THE WORLD, EVEN!
PLANTS HAVE BEEN DISPERSING THEIR SEEDS THROUGH A VARIETY OF MEANS FOR MILLIONS OF YEARS--BY HAVING BIRDS SWALLOW THEM IN THE FORM OF FRUIT--BY ATTACHING TO MAMMALS' FUR ENCASED IN CLINGY BURRS!
I AM MERELY UPDATING THIS SYSTEM!
WHEN THESE PACKAGES GO OUT, THEY'LL BE COVERED IN MILLIONS OF MICROSCOPIC SEEDPODS!
AND WHEREVER THEIR FINAL DESTINATION MAY BE, THOSE SEEDS WILL TAKE ROOT--
AND YOU'LL COVER THE ENTIRE PLANET IN YOUR VINES!
YES... AND BEFORE HUMANITY IS EVEN THE WISER, I WILL BE ABLE TO EXERT MY INFLUENCE OVER EVERY CORNER OF THE GLOBE!
THE REIGN OF ANIMALS OVER THE EARTH IS OVER! I SHALL LEAD THE PLANTS IN THEIR NEW DOMINION OF--
CRASH
EH...?

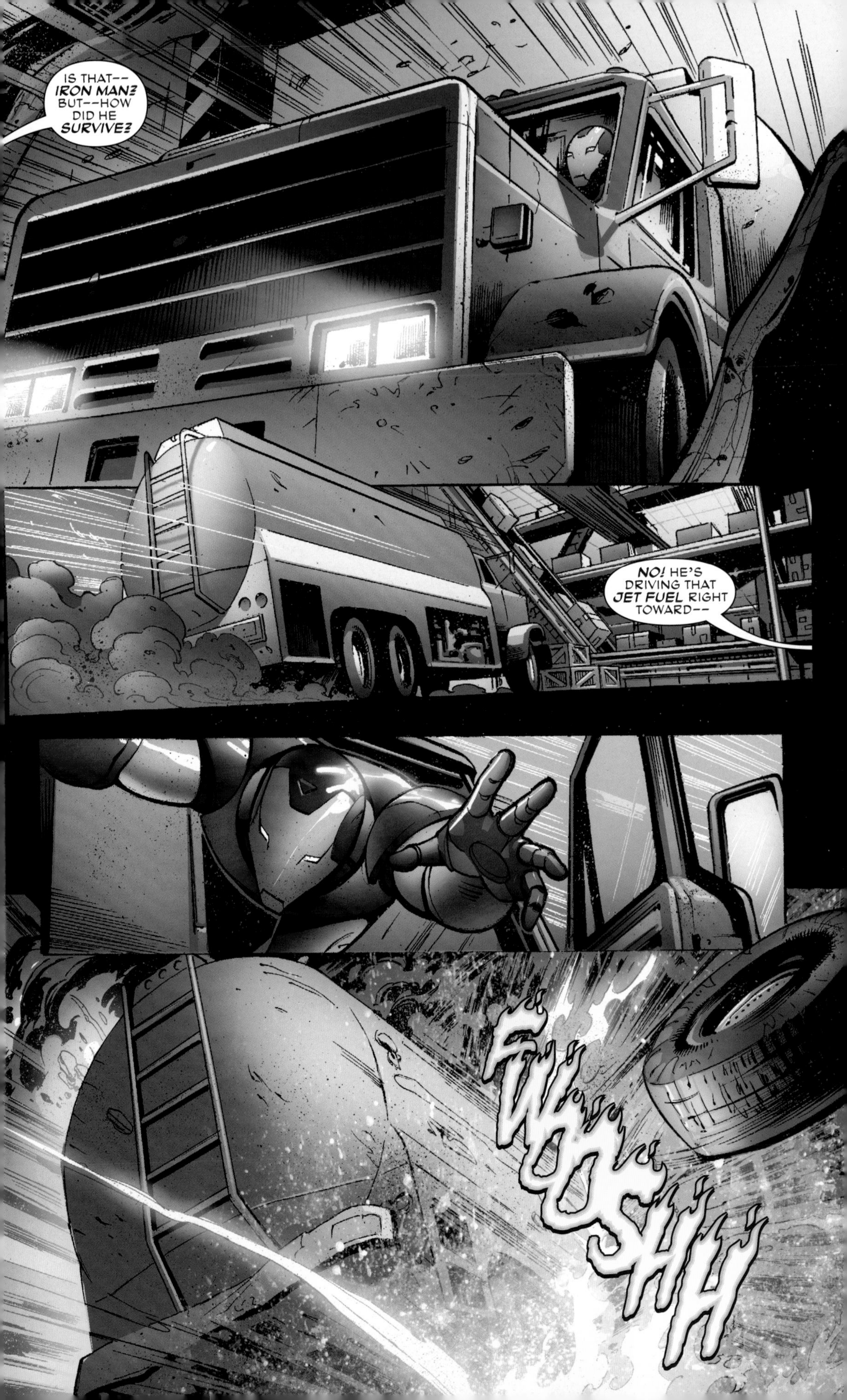
IS THAT--
IRON MAN? BUT--HOW DID HE SURVIVE?
NO! HE'S DRIVING THAT JET FUEL RIGHT TOWARD--
FWOOSHH

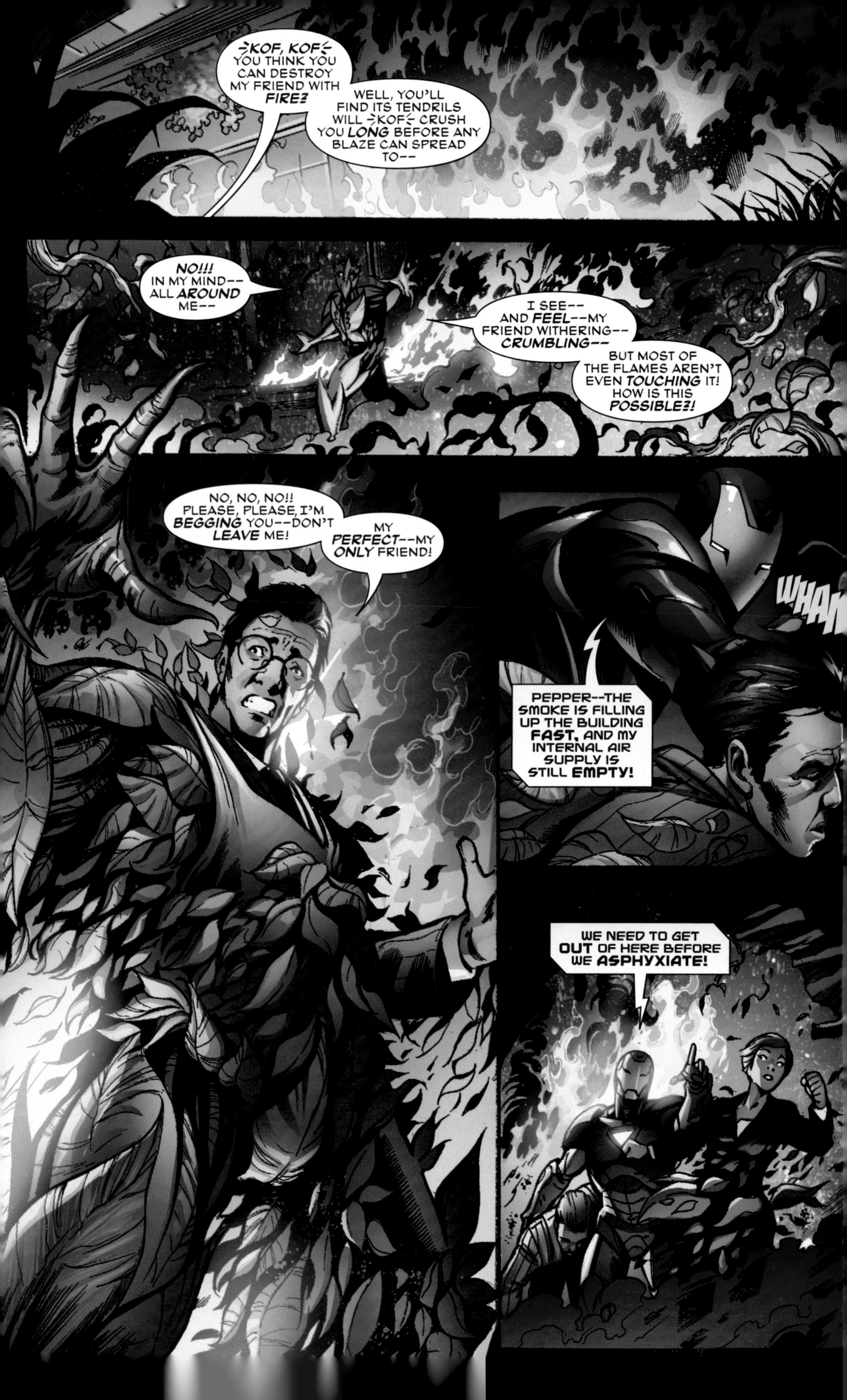

≻KOF, KOF≺ YOU THINK YOU CAN DESTROY MY FRIEND WITH FIRE?
WELL, YOU'LL FIND ITS TENDRILS WILL ≻KOF≺ CRUSH YOU LONG BEFORE ANY BLAZE CAN SPREAD TO--
NO!!! IN MY MIND-- ALL AROUND ME--
I SEE-- AND FEEL--MY FRIEND WITHERING-- CRUMBLING--
BUT MOST OF THE FLAMES AREN'T EVEN TOUCHING IT! HOW IS THIS POSSIBLE?!
NO, NO, NO!! PLEASE, PLEASE, I'M BEGGING YOU--DON'T LEAVE ME!
MY PERFECT--MY ONLY FRIEND!
PEPPER--THE SMOKE IS FILLING UP THE BUILDING FAST, AND MY INTERNAL AIR SUPPLY IS STILL EMPTY!
WE NEED TO GET OUT OF HERE BEFORE WE ASPHYXIATE!

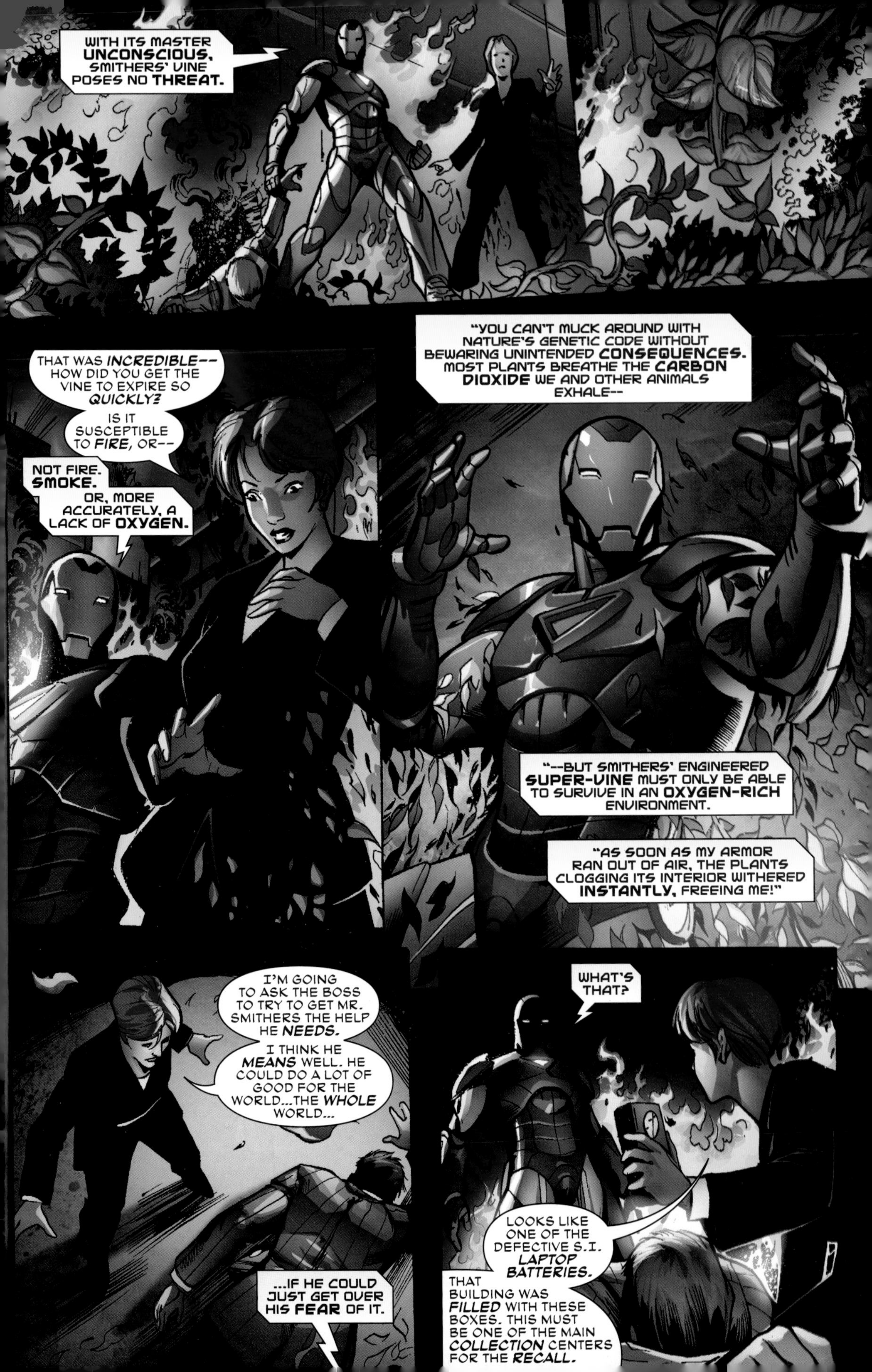
WITH ITS MASTER UNCONSCIOUS, SMITHERS' VINE POSES NO THREAT.
THAT WAS INCREDIBLE-- HOW DID YOU GET THE VINE TO EXPIRE SO QUICKLY?
IS IT SUSCEPTIBLE TO FIRE, OR--
NOT FIRE. SMOKE.
OR, MORE ACCURATELY, A LACK OF OXYGEN.
"YOU CAN'T MUCK AROUND WITH NATURE'S GENETIC CODE WITHOUT BEWARING UNINTENDED CONSEQUENCES. MOST PLANTS BREATHE THE CARBON DIOXIDE WE AND OTHER ANIMALS EXHALE--
"--BUT SMITHERS' ENGINEERED SUPER-VINE MUST ONLY BE ABLE TO SURVIVE IN AN OXYGEN-RICH ENVIRONMENT.
"AS SOON AS MY ARMOR RAN OUT OF AIR, THE PLANTS CLOGGING ITS INTERIOR WITHERED INSTANTLY, FREEING ME!"
I'M GOING TO ASK THE BOSS TO TRY TO GET MR. SMITHERS THE HELP HE NEEDS.
I THINK HE MEANS WELL. HE COULD DO A LOT OF GOOD FOR THE WORLD...THE WHOLE WORLD...
...IF HE COULD JUST GET OVER HIS FEAR OF IT.
WHAT'S THAT?
LOOKS LIKE ONE OF THE DEFECTIVE S.I. LAPTOP BATTERIES.
THAT BUILDING WAS FILLED WITH THESE BOXES. THIS MUST BE ONE OF THE MAIN COLLECTION CENTERS FOR THE RECALL.

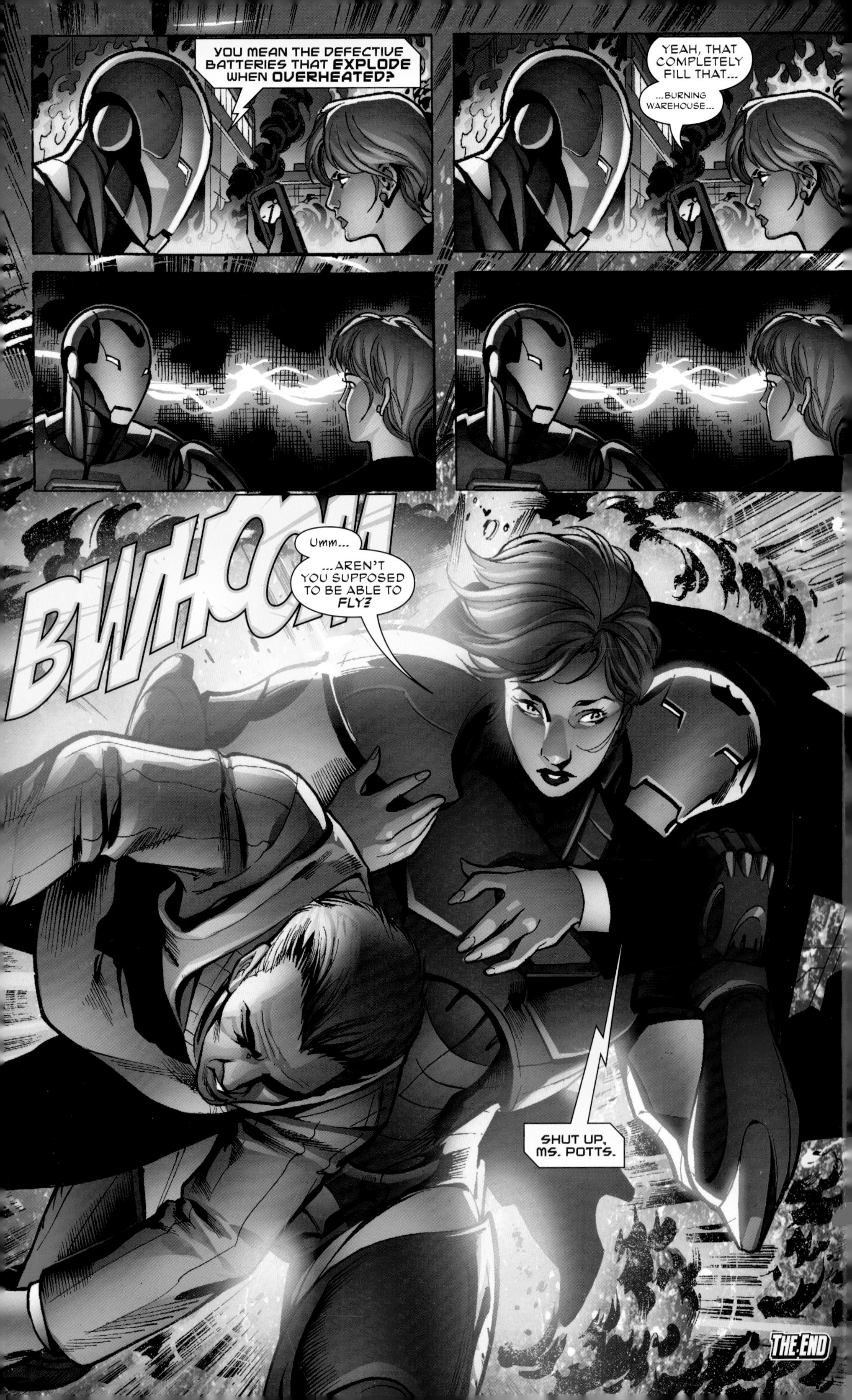
YOU MEAN THE DEFECTIVE BATTERIES THAT EXPLODE WHEN OVERHEATED?
YEAH, THAT COMPLETELY FILL THAT...
...BURNING WAREHOUSE...
BWHOOM
Umm...
...AREN'T YOU SUPPOSED TO BE ABLE TO FLY?
SHUT UP, MS. POTTS.
THE END